Arthur Williams Austin

**The Woman and the Queen**

A Ballad and Other Specimens of Verse

Arthur Williams Austin

**The Woman and the Queen**
*A Ballad and Other Specimens of Verse*

ISBN/EAN: 9783744786690

Printed in Europe, USA, Canada, Australia, Japan

Cover: Foto ©Andreas Hilbeck / pixelio.de

More available books at **www.hansebooks.com**

# THE WOMAN AND THE QUEEN:

## 𝔄 𝔅𝔞𝔩𝔩𝔞𝔡,

AND

## OTHER SPECIMENS OF VERSE.

BY

## ARTHUR W. AUSTIN,

OF WEST ROXBURY, MASS.

CAMBRIDGE:

PRESS OF JOHN WILSON AND SON.

1875.

# PREFACE.

THE outlines of the story of the WOMAN AND THE QUEEN are in the twenty-fourth section of Warton's "History of English Poetry."

Several of the other specimens of verse were published in the "Boston Courier," while under charge of Mr. Lunt.

GENIUS was sent to the Byron Banquet at New York in 1870.

"West Roxbury" is added on the title-page, there being a gentleman of the same name at Buffalo, N.Y., who has published some excellent verse.

The Poems are printed in this more enduring form, for the friends to whom this book is respectfully dedicated.

WEST ROXBURY, Mass.,
        March, 1875.

# CONTENTS.

# THE WOMAN AND THE QUEEN.

IN an age when princes wasted
   Half their lives in contests vain,
Earl Barnard and the German King
   Fought for possession of a plain.

The cost of War it was not worth.
   Oh! when will man delight in Peace!
Whiche'er prevailed, the gain was small,
   And slight his honor would increase.

But these with them of small account,
   And they to battle made appeal:
The Earls and Kings of those old days
   Thought little of the common weal.

The peasant struggled with his fate,
   The nobles warred against the throne.
The age was dark and barbarous, —
   As dark and barb'rous as our own.

The Earl prevailed in border war,
    And many pris'ners bore away.
He held them in his castle keep,
    And kept them there for many a day.


A captive Count he treated well,
    And oft Earl Barnard would unbend ;
And, while the time was drifting on,
    Earl Barnard hailed him as a friend.


And oft they spoke in bant'ring mood,
    When wine right caution had disarmed.
Earl Barnard (he was Glory's slave)
    Had never been by Woman charmed.


The wily Count describes the charms
    That to the German Queen belong, —
Those peerless charms, that matchless grace
    Full oft rehearsed in minstrels' song.


" Ah, never in these wilds of yours,
    Earl Barnard, saw you face so fair :
Well might you give ten years of life
    To see the beauty dwelling there ! "

This wily Count then boldly planned
   That soon a journey should be made,
By which the Earl might see the Queen
   In all her matchless charms arrayed.

And Earl Barnard, much entreated,
   Went, disguised, the Queen to view;
Gave the captive Count his freedom. —
   Often men wrong paths pursue.

And the Count, of faith regardless,
   Sought to bring the Earl to woe;
To the Queen gave information
   How he had ensnared their foe.

But the Queen, with gen'rous feeling,
   Such as noble thought inspires,
First indignantly reproves him,
   Then his silence she requires.

Says: "In your faith the Earl reposes,
   You have taught him to confide.
Nought is gained by treach'rous counsel:
   Truth and Honor are allied!

In this world, if you would prosper,
  Remember, since the birth of time,
No good has come from faithless action :
  Seek not success by heartless crime.

As a Hermit you have brought him :
  Let him go to Holy Mass,
And I there, by chance, may see him
  When the monks and friars pass.

For I like to see the valiant, —
  And Earl Barnard's fame is great, —
Better were he our supporter,
  For divisions cramp a State.

On the morrow to his Highlands
  Then dismiss him, safe from harms ;
Not for worlds would I destroy him,
  Hither lured by fabled charms."

And the Hermit, at the chapel
  Where the holy hymns they sing,
Humbly asking for her bounty,
  From the Queen received a ring.

At this time the King was absent,
　And the Queen had power alone ;
For the King, though brave, was anxious
　For the safety of his throne.

He had said to his bold Barons:
　" To distant region I repair,
And my Queen, both loved and trusted,
　Barons ! she must be your care ! "

But the Barons, in his absence,
　Basely to the Queen proposed.
Though her woman's spirit suffered,
　She their baseness ne'er disclosed.

For those touch the pride of woman,
　Who come near to be denied ; *
And she will resort to silence
　To conceal her wounded pride.

The Barons' malice deep excited,
　To deeper villany they go ;
And they hasten to confine her,
　Lest delay should work them woe.

* Lady Mary Wortley Montagu.

Long the King was absent, distant.
　　Daily, anxious thoughts oppressed ;
And mysterious voices sounded,
　　When at night he sought for rest.

And at length thrice came a vision,
　　Thrice arousing from repose ;
And his Queen was thrice presented
　　As encompassed round with foes.

Thrice the Queen in seeming anguish
　　At his couch in terror stands,
Still in pride of youth and beauty,
　　Stretching forth imploring hands.

By the wondrous vision startled,
　　He no longer made delay,
But, with heart and brain excited,
　　Hastened homeward on his way.

And his thoughts were restless, thrilling,
　　When in sight the palace dome.
Who, long absent, is not anxious,
　　Drawing near the much-loved home ?

And the Queen, so loved and trusted,
   Dearer than the flowers of May,
She, in durance vile, was guarded, —
   Shut from her the joy of day.


Round the King the traitors gathered,
   And with falsehood filled his soul;
That they poisoned at the fountain,
   Over that obtained control.


" Sire, the Queen has been unfaithful,"
   Thus they artfully proclaim,
" Smiled upon a youthful minstrel,
   And your household brought to shame!


Sire, to us was much intrusted:
   (God our fury will forgive!)
We revenged your sullied honor, —
   Know the minion ceased to live!


And, great King! you well remember
   How your counsels she withstood,
When the traitor Earl defied you,
   Backed by all his mountain brood.

Know then, Sire, her guilt and treason, —
    Must we break it to the King ? —
She has seen your foe, Earl Barnard,
    On him has bestowed a ring !

In this Court he rashly ventured, —
    And no power but hers could save, —
And the Queen, his presence knowing,
    False to you, she freedom gave.

And what further passed between them
    Is not fitting here to tell :
It would raise most fearful passion,
    Dangerous and hard to quell."

When the King heard their relation,
    Heard she let his foe depart,
First o'ercome with deep emotion,
    Then fierce rage infects his heart.

Deep the rage of gen'rous natures,
    Stung by unexpected blow,
Stung by hands of those they cherished :
    See proud Ilium wrapt in woe !

Thus deceived by worthless traitors,
 Then his gen'rous spirit broke,
And in frenzy, mad, tempestuous,
 Thus the King in passion spoke:

"O Woman, Woman! ever straying,
 Wayward as the swallow's flight,
Changeful as the hues of morning,
 When blushing clouds shed varied light!

Why should fate bring such disaster
 To a soul so frank as mine?
Why should faith so free, implicit,
 Find a heart so false as thine?

By the blood of all the Cæsars,
 By my father's glorious name,
By the hopes that point hereafter,
 By my mother's spotless fame,

By the wonders of the ocean,
 By the glories of the sky,
By the Christian Gods, and Pagan,
 This false woman soon shall die!"

Thus far : then excess of passion
   Choked his utterance.   In fierce mood,
With jealous anger the attendant,
   He, distraught, a statue stood.

When recovered from his stupor,
   To great wrong was he betrayed ;
For a demon then possessed him,
   And his altered nature swayed.

Said, " Let the morrow see this woman
   In our open court be tried :
Spite of all her subtle counsels,
   By the proofs we will abide ! "

The good Queen, thus basely slandered,
   On her innocence reposed, —
Confident and strong in virtue,
   Though by bars and bolts enclosed.

And the Queen, with few attendants,
   On the morrow did appear ;
By no veil her face was shaded,
   And no look betokened fear.

There she stood in radiant beauty,
　　Not unconscious of her charms ;
Truth in every feature beaming, —
　　Truth and beauty, victor's arms !

On her cheek the blood was mantling,
　　As she calmly viewed the scene ;
And all eyes were turned upon her, —
　　Turned upon the beauteous Queen.

Then the eyes of falsehood glittered,
　　Like subtle serpents charming prey :
When her eye of truth was lifted,
　　Falsehood felt its lightning ray !

When she heard the wrongful charges,
　　For ever meant her fame to blast,
Woman's dignity sustained her,
　　In heart courage unsurpassed.

" O King ! " she said, with voice melodious,
　　In tones all musical and free,
" Never in my faith I faltered,
　　Ne'er was recreant to thee !

This heart alone to thee devoted,
　　Lit with feeling, — Love's pure ray, —
Shall appear as lucid crystal,
　　When these clouds shall break away.

I know well your gen'rous nature,
　　Though you wear remorseless brow ;
But your fame to me is dearer
　　Than the life in peril now.

Well I know your noble nature, —
　　Heaven's own gift when you were born, —
Well I know that noble nature
　　All injustice holds in scorn.

I have seen the famed Earl Barnard,
　　Counted valiant, brave, and true,
At the risk of base espial,
　　And of misconstruction, too.

As a Hermit, he was present
　　In the chapel where they sing,
And I gave the Hermit bounty,
　　From my finger gave a ring.

From that moment I ne'er saw him;
　But the noble knows its own,
And I wished no harm should reach him,
　For the honor of thy throne!

What I gave, I gave in honor,
　All in honor, — not in shame;
What I gave, I gave in honor,
　As a royal Queen became!

I well knew the Knight was noble,
　And foul treachery I restrained,
Which could only have conception
　In a demon disenchained.

Do you ask me why thus tempted
　To observe the hermit Knight?
Ask why rivers run to ocean,
　Or why drifted snow is white!

Ask why winter's winds are piercing,
　Why summer's flowers have rich perfume,
Why has autumn golden fruitage,
　Why in springtime lilies bloom!

Ask why stars, in heaven's concave,
  Beautiful and brightly glow;
Ask why ocean rolls its waters
  In such wond'rous ebb and flow !

Ask why sunward eagles soar, —
  But never think it worth the while
To inquire, or make a question,
  Why valor has a woman's smile !

To see Earl Barnard, passion prompted, —
  Woman's passion at her birth,
Which misled our common mother,
  Who risked Paradise for Earth !

Do you ask why thus I yielded ?
  You know woman's nature well :
That first passion Heaven gave her,
  Ever with her seems to dwell !

Further answer I concede not,
  I shall not myself demean ;
On my former fame relying
  As a Woman, as a Queen !

Think not that I ask for favor!
   Traitors, falsehood I defy!
And my fame shall not be clouded,
   Like a star in darkened sky!

Think not that I ask for favor!
   Traitors, falsehood I defy!
And my fame shall be unclouded,
   As a star in azure sky.

Bring me now to any trial,
   That my faith may proven be;
For my life will have no charm,
   If a wife unworthy thee.

Ever are the base conspiring
   Virtue, truth, to undermine.
With the faithful should be union,
   When the treacherous combine!

Throw that magic mantle round me,
   Which detects unchaste desire!
Try me now by any ordeal
   That the laws of man require!

Throw that wond'rous mantle o'er me,
  And its folds around me furl :
You shall see no quivering motion,
  You shall spy no wavy curl !

God is just, although mysterious :
  On His wisdom I will lean ;
Though in man may be no mercy,
  The God of Heaven protects your Queen !"

Still the King, in frenzied passion,
  Not from evil counsel free,
Still believing the false Barons,
  Issued this unjust decree :

Unless champion 'gainst the Barons
  Will her innocence proclaim,
And in mortal combat foil them,
  She is doomed to cruel flame !

Seven days to raise a champion :—
  Nearly ended was the time.
Craven Barons never hastened
  To proclaim her free from crime.

To the mountains went the story,
   Thither borne by fame or fairy ;
There it roused a noble spirit,
   Brought the eagle from his eyry.

All the courtly priests deserted
   Her who made them what they were.
Curse the priest ! he worse than faithless,
   Who will not for virtue dare.

All the courtly priests deserted
   Her who made them what they were.
But a holy famed Confessor
   To her prison made repair.

In her prison, fearful, anxious,
   Anxious thoughts her mind employ.
But, when summoned to confession,
   She addressed the Saint with joy.

"I am grateful, holy Father,
   That your thought to me was given.
Faithful, I will make confession,
   Freely as I hope for heaven.

To your ear, my kind Confessor,
    All the truth I will relate:
Strange, not wrong but virtuous action
    Brings me to this mournful state.

'Tis a dark and cruel story
    Of a pure wife's slandered name;
And I fear, truth not appearing,
    I shall pass with darkened fame.

Both the Barons that accuse me
    Basely sought my love to gain:
Faithless to their Lord and King,
    Need I say they sought in vain?

And they wickedly pursued me,
    Wickedly pursued in vain:
All their arts they found resisted,
    Only met with high disdain.

To no other ear, Confessor,
    Would I this dark story tell:
In your safe and holy keeping,
    There it must for ever dwell.

The base traitors thought it safer
  To accuse me to the King :
All are slanders, — their invention,
  Save the story of the ring.

Thinking that I best consulted
  My dear husband's highest fame, —
True, I counselled against contest,
  When Earl Barnard made his claim.

It is true I saw Earl Barnard,
  All in singleness of heart ;
It is true I gave the counsel
  That, unharmed, he should depart.

Though my heart in twain is riven,
  Knowing not what may betide,
That the King will lose in honor
  Pains me more than all beside.

Him the traitors have deluded,
  And with poison filled his mind ;
He is altered in his nature,
  Which before was ever kind.

Holy Father, I am fearful,
  Will no ray my soul illume?
Will no brave defender save me
  In life's vigor, in its bloom?"

Then the priest said, "Be of courage!
  God Himself will succor bring:
He will raise for thee the valiant,
  Will restore thee to the King.

Know the weak, in truth, are mighty:
  Keep, my child, a steadfast mind!
Though dark clouds are now obscuring,
  Rays of sunshine are behind!"

Leaving her with words of comfort,
  The holy Father takes his way
To the King in Court assembled:
  Craves he speech without delay.

To the King he then addressed him:
  "Know thy Queen from fault is free!
Live thou on in faith exalted
  That thy wife is worthy thee!"

But the traitors then accused him
　　As suborned the Queen to aid ;
But he boldly met their falsehood,
　　And his presence then displayed.

Though his face a visor shrouded,
　　Through it eyes of eagle gleamed ;
In a moment all were conscious
　　That he was not what he seemed.

From his shoulders dropped the vestment, —
　　For the cowl makes not the monk ;
When he stood a man before them,
　　Craven spirits quickly shrunk.

For the caitiff and the coward,
　　Traitors base, all faithless knaves,
Shrink before the face of manhood :
　　Falsehood's patrons are its slaves !

Then he raised his hand to heaven,
　　And the caitiffs showed alarm,
When they saw the power that rested,
　　That rested in that stalwart arm.

Then he spoke in voice full earnest,
　And his stature seemed to loom,
Daring both to mortal combat,
　In the field to meet their doom.

They, by guilty fears half-conquered,
　Conscious that their guilt was known,
Quickly in the field of combat
　By the Knight were overthrown.

Of the battle I will tell not, —
　Such have been described of yore :
Hurled to earth, the faithless Barons
　Both soon weltered in their gore.

Shouts on shouts from all the people,
　When they witnessed the defeat ;
And then friends appeared, as legion,
　Eager the loved Queen to greet.

In the morning, she was anxious :
　In the evening, comfort found,
Then her praise spoke all the people :
　Often with them such rebound.

Then around the Knight was gathered
  A rejoicing, happy crowd :
Wild with passion, him they greeted,
  Cheered him with their plaudits loud.

Then the Knight, the King approaching,
  From his face the visor drew,
And the people gazed, astounded,
  When Earl Barnard came to view!

But the King, alone surprised not,
  Hailed him with a cordial voice,
And the herald's proclamation
  Bade all heartily rejoice.

Said the King, his right hand waving,
  " King and Earl no more are foes,
King and Earl in firm alliance,
  In the brave the wise repose !

Now I know the Queen is truthful,
  To the winds all passion fling.
Now I know Earl Barnard faithful,
  And Earl Barnard knows the King.

As I know Earl Barnard faithful,
  I now place him at the helm :
I proclaim him Lord High Steward, —
  This is safety to the realm !

I, unknown, unseen, was present,
  When the Queen confession made.
And her truthfulness and kindness
  All my jealous rage allayed.

To the Queen I bow full humbly,
  Freely my injustice own.
To my bosom now most welcome,
  Dear, loved partner of my throne !"

Then the Queen with joy was lifted
  From the shades of deepest night,
Looking upward, joyous springing
  To a day of golden light.

Such is Woman, my dear reader,
  Ray of light, approved above !
All forgiving, — all forgiving, —
  All they pardon, where they love !

# GENIUS.

A ND what is Genius ? answer all who feel :
    To Burns, to Dante, Byron, all appeal.
And where is genius of the highest grade ?
In Shakespeare's urn, with lofty Milton's shade ;
Mild it reposes in sage Franklin's tomb ;
Its sleep was restless in Helena's gloom ;
It dwelt with Homer on the Grecian shore,
There long resided, but resides no more.
There, other names the classic mem'ry calls,
Embraced in Sparta, Thebes, and Athens' walls ;
There swarming bees on Pindar's lips repose,
There Love immortal with Anacreon glows ;
One in heroic strains of heroes sung,
And on their laurels vernal lustre flung ;
One crowned with roses touched a harp divine,
Tuning its strings in praise of Love and Wine ;
And, though the tide of time has flowed so long,
Each stands unrivalled in his realm of song.

Forsaking Greece, Genius, with hopeful eye,
Turned to the West and sought Hesperia's sky.
In Latian land it found a welcome home,
Virgil and Horace honored ancient Rome ;
In Latian lands it made a long delay,
And lengthened ages lightened with its ray.
Genius itself stood wondering in amaze,
When it confronted Ariosto's gaze,
Saw in his eyes poetic frenzy roll,
His lightning smile, — the lightning of the soul,
When with creative power he poured along
The magic music of his varied song ;
And mind burst forth in streams and rushing rills,
As mountain torrents speed from crested hills,
When Spring in triumph loosens Winter's chain,
And sends the waters leaping to the plain.
    In sculptor's art oft Genius rose supreme,
Illumed the canvas, lit the poet's dream !
Its impulse lent to heighten all that skill
And earnest labor wrought with earnest will.
Though sometimes darkness seemed the sky to shroud,
Its fitful flashes pierced the densest cloud.
Leaving the land that charms youth's waking dreams,
Bright land of sunny skies and classic streams.

Erratic Genius, in its march sublime,
Sought Alfred's bosom in another clime.
Then waked to warmth in Spenser's fairy lay ;
Missed Dryden's youth, but fired his later day ;
Then " glorious John " to Shadwell gave his due ;
With well-poised wit the subtile Shaftsbury drew,
And St. Cecilia's strain and flowing line
Burst forth in floods of "energy divine."
It breathed with Pope in grotto and in grove,
Whene'er he chose in fancy's realms to rove,
Whene'er he sang of glory or of love.
There glows a spirit Earth cannot control,
When Genius is the master of the soul :
How fierce it gleamed within that eye of fire,
When Rousseau leagued with fancy to conspire.
We see its vigor in the potent page,
When Godwin pictures ·dark, relentless rage ;
In Voltaire's calm and cold sarcastic power,
In Cromwell's art, in Tasso's furious hour.
The voice of Genius, in its varied tones,
Has startled monarchs and has shaken thrones.
  Hard to select from England's noble throng
The names that most are consecrate to song.
To group the host that Genius calls its own,
The time allows not now ; but, on its throne,

A noble chief from Scotia's land we hail,
Whom all must honor, and none dare assail.
We call to mind dear Scott, impressing youth
With Jeanie's virtue and Rebecca's truth,
He who in verse and in his fiction drew
The forms of virtue with a pencil true,
And with that pencil scrupled not to trace
The crimes and follies of the kingly race ;
Whose stream as pure as purest fountain flowed,
Whilst in his pages genial fervor glowed ;
Who firm remained, although he saw depart
The cherished visions of his princely heart ;
He who the old delighted, charmed the young,
Must not be left "unhonored and unsung."
But what is Genius without passion's force
To call it forth and prompt it to discourse ?
Genius when warm, inspired by loving eyes,
Is waked to life, aspires to glory's prize.
The love of glory, and the fear of shame,
Have started Genius in a sluggish frame :
The lively wish to reach beyond the hour,
To seize and hold the height of mortal power,
Has brought reposing strength to action high,
And man has soared till dull was fancy's eye.

Passions give strength, though sometimes they mis-
    lead ;
But without passion none can e'er succeed.
The eye of dulness never can see clear,
Starting at shadows, ere the forms appear ;
The soul of dulness never can decide
What should be sought or what be left untried.
By passion's eagle eye is Genius fired,
Genius itself by passion is inspired ;
And it must feel before it can portray
The varied passions that the bosom sway.
The love of glory must the breast inspire,
The love of fame excite with sharp desire,
Ere the full promptings of the soul begin
To seek their vent, or restless work within.
The bard who dwells 'mid storms and rugged climes
Will paint black tempests in his rugged rhymes ;
But he whose eyes on smiling valleys rest
Will dream that calm reposes in each breast.
But Genius' efforts, words that never die,
Present no beauty to the vulgar eye ;
Genius, though great, cannot to churls impart
The spirit, grandeur, of a high-toned heart.
The eagle quells the falcon, — upward borne,
The monarch bird the kestrel holds in scorn.

Envy and Cant most wisely would surmise
That in street fights great Homer lost his eyes;
Suggest, from Juan we should never quote;
That Junius, Junius' letters never wrote;
That Milton's daughters ever lived in fear;
And Shakespeare spent his youth in stealing deer.
Let Envy carp and vulgar Malice rant,
The eye of wisdom penetrates their cant.
Genius survives the cavils of the day,
And lights the future with resplendent ray:
Milton and Shakespeare still adorn the throne,
That Genius raises to its sons alone;
Around their urns the brightest rays serene
With crystal light illuminate the scene.
The roll of ages will not leave a gloom
O'er Homer's ashes or on Byron's tomb:
Genius itself their glory shall sustain,
Their names inscribing in its noblest fane,
On a high column placed, to last as long
As time shall last or man delight in song.

# FANCY.

"In early days the lyric muse could please :
I courted fancy then, in strains like these ;
And fancy's self the language did inspire,
As thus I dashed my fingers o'er the lyre."

COME, fancy, let me waken,
 And let me try my wing :
My courage is unshaken,
 And glows as fresh as spring.
The earth hath lofty mountains,
 And shady valleys deep,
Where streams and gentle fountains
 In quiet murmurs creep ;
And forests which are waving
 With pines of branches vast,
And oaks whose boughs are braving
 The rudest wintry blast.
And as o'er earth we travel,
 Amid its boundless range,
Its mysteries to unravel,
 Or view its frequent change,

What quick thoughts will be flying,
   Swifter than eagle's wing,
E'en fancy's self defying,
   As thought to thought will spring !
Through earth the streams are flowing
   Which lighten labor's toil,
The clouds, their rain bestowing,
   Will fertilize the soil ;
But those rich streams unheeded
   Flow when the clouds deny, —
Aye, when they most are needed,
   Earth's life-blood they supply.
The stars, in distance roaming,
   To other shores are bright,
And gladden some far gloaming
   With their celestial light.
Beneath the depths of ocean
   Are treasures vast and deep ;
Unrocked by any motion,
   In calm repose they sleep.
And jewels have been glowing
   Beneath earth's surface deep,
And fountains have been flowing
   Through channels rough and steep.

Those fountains have been streaming
   For ever on their way,
The diamonds have been gleaming,
   Though hid from light of day.
And lofty thoughts are rushing
   Through each immortal mind,
Beneath its surface gushing
   Mysterious, undefined ;
Until some object rouses,
   Which seems to be of worth,
Some call the soul espouses,
   Which brings its action forth.
'Yes, when the tempest rages,
   Those powers, before concealed,
Its fury then engages,
   Then courage is revealed.
Harmonious streams are gliding
   For ever through the soul,
 And joyous there abiding,
   Through its recesses roll.
Melodious strains there ranging,
   Which never will depart,
With chimes for ever changing, —
   They cheer the human heart.

# POMPEII.

A WANDERER 'mid Pompeii's ruin stands,
   Viewing the scene with not incurious eye.
Strange desolation! marks of pride are left,
Emblems that tell of human vanity,
And some which shadow baser passions still.
But here not long he meditates ; his thought
Dwells not on those who long have passed away :
Still, as he treads among the ancient graves,
He makes some question of the tenants there.
   Was it good fortune or an evil fate
Sent to this urn the graceful form of youth,
In woman's loveliness, in beauty's strength,
When ruddy beauty heightened beauty's blush ?
Good fortune may have snatched from wretchedness,
Or happiness been wrecked by evil fate !
   Or was it one sporting in childish years,
Whose destined hours in tenderness had flown
Amid the charms affection sheds on life,
That here has long reposed ?   Who left this world

With faith consummate on the mind impressed,
Unchanging truth still in the form enthroned ;
But, early passing on from earth to heaven,
The seal of death imprinted on the brow,
Ere time and passion wrote their victories !
　Or was the one that lies inurnèd here,
Cut off by fate before he reached the goal
Which his ambition hailed as worthy thought?
And, his career not furnishing that fame
To which the ardent vainly oft aspire,
Does he in death still wrestle with vain dreams
Of what he was, or what he would have been ?
'Mid fearful nightmare and terrific pain,
Perchance this tomb to him is but a prison,
No rest within the grave ; ambitious still
To leave bright record in the universe.
　Perhaps a miscreant foul, from miscreant sprung,
Marked at the start by the Almighty hand,
Beyond all doubt, all question, all dispute,
As fit for every vice that man abhors,
Here long has ceased to rot, whose boundless crimes
Exceeded all the crimes of his vile race,
Though all his race surpassed in crime before ;
A shameless coward and consummate knave,

Ready to pilfer, murder, or to steal,
By Satan lent to disarray the world,
A country and all human rights betray.
On such a wretch scorn piled on scorn were vain :
Earth's justice never could such villain reach, —
Immortal God alone could judge his doom.

    Perchance, some patriot reposes here,
Who loved his country and maintained its cause,
Watched its career in much of thoughtful hope,
Contended manfully against its fall,
But knew its danger, and that danger warned ;
Ardent to aid, conscious he could not save,
Saw fell corruption sapping all its strength ;
Seeing its downward course, foresaw its doom,
Not fearing outward foes, but those within,
In bitterness of spirit and of heart,
Its inward would have hurled to hell's own door,
And hell would darker grow at their approach !

    Haply this may have been a suffering wretch,
To whom the grave was but a welcome friend,
The arms of death a refuge long desired.

    Or yet this may have been sweet fancy's child,
That lived within his own created sphere,
Fearfully proud, nicely fastidious,

Holding within his breast high hopes, high thoughts,
That, never brought.to light, not noted down,
Have perished in their beauty.   Over such
The Muses hover, and they know their child ;
They feed him with the fancies that beguile,
They smooth his path through life, and, when he
     sleeps,
In thoughtful music chant his requiem.
   Whoe'er the tenants were, by fortune blest,
It gave them to the earth's tranquillity,
Ere the volcano burst in sweeping flame:
The dead were better than the living then !

# JUPITER AND HEBE.

"DAUGHTER, I am growing old!
    And my blood flows faint and cold;
From my arm the nerve has gone,
From my limbs the strength has flown;
Faltering are my weary feet,
And my pulses scarcely beat.
Life immortal was my boon:
Must I wane, like yon pale moon?
Power immortal mine alone:
Must I quit this starry throne?
Yield this canopy of earth,
Star-gemmed at proud Juno's birth?
'Mid this canopy of blue
Then the living lightnings flew,
Startling with their piercing ray
What is now the Milky Way.
Oh, the grandeur of that night!
At the intervening light,

Beaming brightly, high, serene,
The lost Pleiad last was seen.
Storm and lightning wildly raged ;
Both how quickly were assuaged !
Juno's eye and towering form
Calmed the lightning, quelled the storm.
Storm and tempest soon were still,
Both resolved at Juno's will.
Iris came with rainbow dyes,
Signing peace to earth and skies ;
Always welcome to the wise.
Peace with wisdom ever runs :
War, a demon, wisdom shuns.
All will find, as years increase,
Peace is wisdom, wisdom peace.

I am faint and sick and weak.
Health once mantled on this cheek.
From this brow, and from this face,
Fled have dignity and grace.
If thou aid not, I've no choice
But to court Oblivion's voice !

Daughter, fly ! thy father aid,
Heal the ravage time has made,

Pluck the silver from my brow ;
Let not age steal o'er me now.
The golden moments, as they flow,
All that's fair and good bestow.
Bid Apollo bring his light,
To relume his father's sight.
Call the powers that sway the air,
Hither let each grace repair.
Let Minerva do her share :
She had wisdom at her birth,
And the olive gave to Earth ;
Life prolonger, and the queen
Of a field of thought serene.
Bring a laver of fresh dew,
Mountain roses round me strew,
Honey from Hymettus bring,
Rich with violets of spring,
Or with summer's sweetest flowers,
Blooming in Hesperian bowers.
Call Terpsichore's maidens fair,
Mountain nymphs, with flowing hair,
Hearts untouched by earthly care,
Lips that breathe with fond desire,
Eyes that love might well inspire,

When they throw a laughing glance
Round their comrades in the dance.
Let the Muse, with lute in hand,
Crowned with laurel, lead the band.

Bring the laughing Hours along!
Cheer my heart with flowing song!
Who existence would desire,
If denied the mirthful lyre?
Bring a cup of rosy wine,
Rich as that young blush of thine,
Touch it with thy lips divine,
Lips disclosing crystalline:
I will press it then to mine.
Smooth this brow, renerve this arm,
Prove each limb with potent charm,
All thy genius round me fling;
Turn this winter to life's spring;
Give the life that morning brings,
When young eagles try their wings;
Give me, give me radiant life;
Better that, with ceaseless strife,
Than the late and dreary past
With spectral shadows overcast.

Give me of thy glowing breath,
And thy arms around me wreathe;
Let thy joyous, beating heart
Life and youth and strength impart."

Hebe, beautiful and true,
Doth her father's strength renew,
All with filial love refined,
Joyful, meets the task assigned.

" Hebe, ask a boon from me,
I will grant it cheerfully.
Fond and gentle, pure, thou art,
Graced with beauty, high of heart ;
And thy modest, blooming face,
Full of sweetness and of grace,
Shows of passion sign nor trace.
Child, thy heart is fresh and green,
Like the grass in sylvan scene
After showers have passed away,
In the time of flowery May.
All the hopes that round thee cling
Joyous are, as breath of spring,
When the birds are on the wing,
When in rivalry they sing ;

All the fears that round thee crowd
Lighter than yon sun-gilt cloud,
Which is fading fast away
'Neath Apollo's burning ray.
Richer is that blush of thine
Than the gleam of sparkling wine.
Now! I see the cheerful ray
That foretells the break of day.

All I am to thee I owe!
What on thee shall I bestow?
Age has ceased, and with it pain:
Daughter, I am young again.

What is greater, then, in truth
Than the bloom of glorious youth?
Thou art bashful, in thine eyes
Is the glow of sweet surprise,
On thy heaving breast the flush
That adorns a virgin blush.
What of wealth or what of fame
Is it worth thy while to claim?
Daughter, I will choose for thee:
Youth and health thy portion be!

On thee youth and health attend,
And thy power shall have no end.
Youth immortal I bestow,
Health and youth in hand shall go,
Long as ceaseless ages flow.
And this power to thee is given
Over all the gods of heaven.
Neptune from his watery waste
Will to thy glad presence haste ;
And that darker god below,
Whose grim visage pictures woe,
Would be glad to lose his throne,
Could he make thy gift his own !
And thy bridal, it shall be
All that may be worthy thee.
Our wayward Juno cease to frown,
Thee Juno's self with flowers shall crown ;
And, once profuse, her hands supply
Wreaths to engarland all the sky ;
Youth, Beauty, Courage, be allied
When Hebe blooms a happy bride.

Give my sceptre of command,
Let me wield it in this hand.

What a front, and what a brow !
Juno would not know me now.
How these ringlets graceful flow !
How my inmost pulses glow !
Ages now have rolled in vain :
Jupiter is young again ! "

## DEIFICATION OF JULIUS CÆSAR.

FROM OVID.

APOLLO'S son,* though alien, God we called!
    In his own city Cæsar was installed!
And though for skill in arts and arms renowned,
For civil wisdom, wars with triumphs crowned,
And rapid conquests of exalted fame,
Augustus' father was his proudest claim!
And aided more amid celestial race,
In the bright throng of stars to fix his place.
And of all Julius' acts we witness bear,
The greatest when he made Augustus heir.
Was it a greater boast his triumphs famed,
Or those great acts when triumphs were unclaimed
Was it a greater glory to defeat
The sea-encircled Britain, bear his fleet
Triumphant through the channels of the stream
Of paper-bearing Nile, or to redeem
And add to Roman state Numidia's coast,
With swelling Pontus, Mithridates' boast,

* Æsculapius.

Than to adopt a great man to preside?
Abundantly for all the Gods provide!
That from no mortal our own prince should rise,
Great Julius was translated to the skies.
　All beauteous Venus then, with features pale,
Saw armed assassins Vesta's priest assail,
Foresaw his mournful death, exclaimed : " O see
The weight of woe, ye Gods, prepared for me!
See, with what deep design the life is sought
Of my sole Julian hope from Troas brought!
Shall I alone be singled from the rest?
Shall I alone with cruel cares be pressed?
Tydides' spear my burning thought recalls,
And next I mourned Troy's ill defended walls ;
I've seen my son to distant regions sped,
On Ocean tossed, among the silent dead,
Doomed then in strife with Turnus to engage,
Or, truth to tell, confronting Juno's rage.
Why call to mind past anguish of my race,
Since present ills all former ills efface?
The sacred fires of Vesta will not glow,
If the dear blood of Vesta's priest shall flow ;
You see ungodly swords, avert this crime,
Forbid the blow, ye Gods! nor let it darken time! "

Venus with troubled mind makes this appeal,
And all the Gods a deep compassion feel ;
And, though unable fate to overthrow,
Present no doubtful signs of future woe.
Trumpets and clarions send from heaven alarms,
Amid dark clouds are heard resounding arms.
The sun's sad spectre sheds a ghastly light,
To warn the world of violated right.
Amid the stars, bright fires were seen to blaze,
And drops of blood, in storms, oft met the gaze ;
Dusky the morning star appeared to view,
And Luna's car had stains of blood-red hue. '
Around the city ghosts in silence creep,
In thousand places ivory statues weep ;
The city through, dogs made nocturnal howls,
Came mournful omens from infernal owls ;
In sacred groves strains of enchantment sound,
And threatening words reverberate around ;
The Gods unsatisfied, though victims bled,
Whose opened entrails showed a wounded head ;
Great tumults by the fibres were made known,
By startling earthquakes troubles were foreshown.
Not all these warnings from the Gods could prove
A bar to treason, nor the fates could move.

The place for crime the Senate House affords,
And in the temple traitors draw their swords.
Then Venus beat her breast with either hand,
And in a cloud to hide her hero planned.
Paris eluded thus Atrides' hate,
By this device Æneas baffled fate.

    And then her father, speaking, said : " My child,
Hope you to master fate ? such hope is wild.
Yourself may enter where the sisters three
Engrave on metal fore-ordained decree.
Secure from thunder and all other shock,
There, on perennial, adamantine rock,
Stamped by the fateful sisters, you may trace
The various fortunes of your favored race.
I read, remember, and will now relate,
That you may know the fixed decrees of fate.
Your great descendant, having filled on earth
The length of days allotted at his birth,
Shall now ascend, acknowledged be in heaven,
Shall find on earth in temples worship given.
And his own son, his heir shall stand alone,
A city's burdens on his shoulders thrown ;
The Gods propitious, well to him belongs
The brave avenging of his father's wrongs.

And conquered Mutina shall seek for peace,
Phillippi's contest shall his fame increase ;
Great Pompey's son, thought master of the waves,
Shall fly the waters that Sicilia laves ;
And Egypt's Queen, the Roman's ill-starred bride,
In vain shall question what the fates decide.
Your Rome shall stand, Canopus hold in awe,
And Rome to Egypt give unquestioned law.
Why should I mention the Barbaric ground,
Or distant countries waves of ocean bound ?
All earth contains shall his dread voice obey,
And the deep seas shall recognize his sway.
At peace the empire, when his mind is free,
Laws he shall shape, shall order just decree ;
Shall turn to civil rule his active mind,
And by his standard morals be refined ;
Regardful of the future, shall engage
His loved wife's son to guide succeeding age ;
Nor shall he reach among the stars his place,
Nor seats celestial shall he ever grace,
Until with Nestor's years his life is crowned,
Then not alone shall earth his glory bound.
  My child ! now seize the spirit of this soul,
And bear your hero far from earth's control ;

Make him a star ; then from his lofty home
The forum he shall view, each burnished dome
Which now, or which hereafter, graces Rome !"
   These words scarce uttered, Venus, Love's own
       Queen,
Stood in the Senate, though by all unseen,
And from great Cæsar snatched the parting soul,
To place among the Gods, among the stars enroll.
And, while she bore, it luminous became,
With fires it glittered, kindled then to flame ;
It sprang above the moon to seek its place,
And lustrous light adorned ethereal space.
   He shines a star benignant ; and the deeds
His son performs, with earnest joy concedes
Superior to his own, while gen'rous fame,
Although the son opposed, confirms the claim.
Great Agamemnon paled his father's fires,
Achilles, Theseus, both surpassed their sires.
More just example I shall now propose,
Jove's star ascendant over Saturn's rose ;
Jove rules above with undisputed sway,
And his behests three mighty realms obey ;
The earth he gave Augustus, to his race,
Thus heaven and earth enjoy an equal grace ;

Both fathers, that with wisdom govern all,
One rules celestial sphere, one this terrestrial ball.
  Grant, O ye Gods, that with Æneas came,
Through whom he triumphed over sword and flame ;
Grant, household Gods, and Romulus our sire,
With the chaste Vesta bearing sacred fire,
Vesta and Phœbus in your hallowed home,
Beneath the roof that crowns our Cæsar's dome,
And Mars, who gave to Rome its warlike powers,
Great Jove, controlling the Tarpeian towers,
All other Gods to whom is rev'rence due, —
O grant this earnest prayer preferred to you :
Grant, all ye Gods, who hear your poet's song,
Far, far beyond my life with grace prolong
His stay on earth, who tempers all so well,
Late let him wish in starry home to dwell ;
He thence shall glance from realms of upper air,
Smiling propitious to his people's prayer.

### PERORATION.

The work I've finished — elements of air,
And fire and sword, and wasting time will spare ;
When that day comes, and come we know it must,
When this strong frame shall be resolved in dust,

Immortal I shall rise o'er stars divine,
And, leaving earth, an honored name be mine.
Where'er Rome's legions are to conquest led,
My name shall flourish, and my verse be read.
Unless a poet's presages are vain,
My fame through ages, glowing, shall remain.

# TRANSLATIONS FROM THE LATIN.

### REGIANUS.

#### Descriptio Loci Amœni.

HERE summer shade the noble plane-tree spreads,
　　Here the tall pines expand their waving heads ;
Here, trembling cypress, bay with berries crowned,
Unite, diffusing welcome shade around.
The wand'ring waters, whirling as they roam,
Flow swiftly o'er the stones in streams of foam.

Place for love's whispers ! here the tuneful bird;
Lover of woods, the nightingale is heard ;
Here sportive swallows skim the flow'ry plains,
And charm with cheerful voice the maids and swains.

## VOMANUS.

### Gardens.

YE Muses, born of Jove, assist my verse!
  The Garden's beauties let me now rehearse:
How oft the garden healthful viands yields,
With choicest fruits from cultivated fields,
Sweet colewort, herbs, and many kinds of roots,
And blooming grapes, and trees with rarest fruits.
Useful and pleasant being well combined,
Thus we enjoy a pleasure most refined.
When a clear stream of murmuring water flows
On furrowed cornfields, moisture it bestows.
And flowers bright gleaming 'mid the varied lawn
With twinkling charms the verdant plain adorn.
The pleasing bees send forth their humming sound
On tops of flowers, or where fresh dews abound.
The elms are burdened with the fruitful vine,
And round the posts the shady vine leaves twine.
The trees wide spread afford us shady bowers,
Their foliage shielding from the noonday hours.
The chatt'ring birds a sweet tide pour along,
Soothing the ears with their melodious song.

Thus gardens cheer, attract, hold in delight,
Give the limbs vigor, captivate the sight,
Lighten the troubles which distress mankind,
And shield from anguish the afflicted mind.
In many ways great joy their culture yields,
When labor finds return in grateful fields.

### Epitaph on a Dog.

I BARKED at thieves, when lovers came was mute:
This did the master and the mistress suit!

### MENANDER AND TERENCE.

Translated from the Latin of TANAQUIL FABER (the father of Madame Dacier),
and prefixed to his edition of Terence, 1671.

THE Graces, mourning, were with grief depressed,
    Life having left Menander's sacred breast;
His spirit wafted to Elysian shore,
They traverse valleys, groves, and mountains o'er,
With cheeks suffused with tears; and, full of woes,
They seek new seats, new temples for repose.
    When Venus saw the Graces thus in grief,
Their labor vain, she sought to give relief;

With foresight blessed, her honeyed mouth outflows
With words like these, their spirits to compose:
  " My dear companions, and my faithful train,
Without whose presence all my gifts are vain,
Receive, ye Graces, comfort, thus distressed,
Great is your loss, and great by all confessed;
But from your hearts dispel all anxious fears,
Although the loss has well deserved our tears.
Live on, live on! there come yet better days:
When thrice ten lustres Phœbus sheds his rays,
And with his shining car enlivens earth,
In distant Carthage dawns a poet's birth.
This poet hailing from the Afric shore,
And none more pleasing to the world before,
Gladly your former honors will restore.
He will rebuild the temples, now o'erthrown,
When future times Menander's verse disown;
Nor will he fear the taunt of envious knave,
Nor the dread sweep of time's encroaching wave;
But his fresh efforts, meeting constant praise,
Will flourish more as onward roll the days.
When time the Grecian drama shall confound,
With Afric verse the playhouse shall resound.
  We then, we then, dear Graces, will perceive,
With so much good, how little cause to grieve."

From TANAQUIL FABER'S edition of Terence : —

SACRUM Menandri pectus
Aura jam reliquerat,
Vagulaque animula
Elysias penetrarat oras.
Tum dolore percitæ,
Virgineasque
Suffusæ lacrymis genas,
Huc et illuc cursitarunt
Perque lucos, perque montes,
Perque vallium sinus,
Cursitarunt Gratiæ,
Quærentes sibi
Queis nova sedibus
Templa ponere possent.

Illas aligeri
Dulcis mater Amoris
Languidasque, fessulasque
Cum videret irritum
Suscepisse laborem.
Tales, futuri provida temporis,
Nectareo Dea
Fudit ore loquelas.

O mihi perpetuæ comites, mihi turba fidelis,
  'Queis sine nec possit ipsa placere Venus :
Accipite, ô Divæ, subiti solatia casus,
  Perculsoque gravem ponite corde metum.
Magna quidem, fateor, clades, ingensque ruina est,
  Quæ possit lacrymas et meruisse meas :
Sed, Divæ, durate tamen, durate, puellæ,
  Sera etenim reddet, sed meliora, dies.
Namque ubi ter denis explerit tempora lustris
  Phœbus, sidereas dum teret axe rotas ;
Nascetur vobis Afra de gente sacerdos,
  Quo nullus toto gratior orbe fuit.
Is vestros olim scriptis reparabit honores,
  Restituetque suis subruta templa locis.
Quin et longa dies delebit scripta Menandri,
  Et quandoque levis carmina pulvis erunt.
Verum Afris scriptis, queis læta theatra sonabunt,
  Tempora qui possit ponere nullus erit
Usque nova nam laude recens Fabella vigebit,
  Nec metuet lepidis invida secla jocis.
Tunc, ô, tunc, Divæ, mecum dicetis et ipsæ,
  Quantula sunt quantis damna repensa bonis !

# TRANSLATIONS FROM THE GREEK ANTHOLOGY.

### ARION.

HAIL, chief of Gods ! whose trident sways alone
    The sea-encircled earth ; whom waves obey,
And all the waters of the teeming deep,
    Where swimming monsters swift in circles play,
And music-loving dolphins lightly leap,—
    Sea-nurslings of the Nereids divine,
Who as a mother Amphitrite own,
    The wife of Neptune from great Tethys' line.
When faithless sailors doomed a wat'ry grave,
    And heartless cast me in dark purple wave,
And I was drifting in Sicilia's bay,
        Me, rough-necked, flat nosed, crooked-back dolphins
            bore,
Furrowing the surface of the trackless way,
    To Tæn'rus' welcome port, on Pelops' shore !

## ANTIPATER.

WHEN pirates slew him on wild desert shore,
  A cloud of cranes did Ibycus implore
To witness bear, the cruel deed proclaim.
Nor did he pray in vain, Erynnis came.
The lucre-loving race no rights revere,
Nor ever hold avenging Gods in fear.
They were convicted in Sisyphia's land,
Where cranes with clamor punishment demand.
Egisthus killed a poet ; and the eye
Of black veiled Furies, vainly sought to fly.

---

FARMER Archippus, by disease oppressed,
About to die, his children thus addressed :
" My children dear, the plough, the spade, employ,
And for my sake a rustic life enjoy ;
Avoid the dangers and the treach'rous breeze
And toilsome labors of the stormy seas.
A mother's more than stepdame's love we crave,
So earth more precious than the surging wave."

---

THOUGH Plato's body in the earth recline,
  His soul is happy with the Gods divine.

His life divine the distant nations own,
His daily life with daily beauty shone:
The good are honored wheresoever known.

———oo;o;oo———

## DIOTIMUS.

### Antæus and Hercules.

THE son of Neptune and the son of Jove
    In youthful, brave and wrestling contest strove.
No brazen vessel the reward of strife,
But a pure struggle for the prize of life.
Antæus crushed by Jove's immortal son,
By Greece, not Libya, was the combat won !

———oo;o;oo———

## RUFINUS.

TRULY there are Graces four,
    Counting her that I adore.
Themis, Pallas, have combined
Her to gift with arts refined :
Lip persuasive, speaking eye,
She with Beauty's Queen can vie ;
In her voice hear Music's powers ;
Her step is like the vernal Hours.

### On my Mistress.

With lips persuasive, speaking eyes,
With Beauty's Queen my Doris vies ;
The vernal Hours with her rejoice ;
Calliope has lent her voice ;
Themis, Minerva, have combined
To gift with art, exalt her mind.
And truly we have Graces four,
Counting the mistress I adore !

### Derkulis.

Two Venuses, four Graces, ten Muses we have here :
A Grace, a Muse, a Venus in Derkulis appear !

### Rhodope.

Rhodope, proud in beauty, my salutation dares deride,
Spurning my garlands from her gate, in the tempest
of her pride.
Now, age and wrinkles, quickly come, quickly hasten
to invade ;
For only you can have the power to humanize this
maid !

RHODA, Rhodope, Mellita, all fair,
Made me a judge their beauties to compare:
Like Goddesses, conspicuous they stood,
And only wanted the nectarean blood.
Remembering Paris, suffering Troja's fall,
As all divine I quickly crowned them all!

---

### MEONIS.

PALLAS and Juno, when my girl they spied,
Both said the shepherd's judgment we abide;
Now Beauty's prize let Meonis obtain,
For conquered twice, if we contest again!

---

RHODA, to thee I send a garland, wove
From flowers late gathered by these hands of mine.
Here lily, celandine, and budding rose,
The tender daffodil, the violet blue.
When crowned with these, abate thy lofty pride:
Thyself, the flowers, the garland, all will fade.

## SIMMIAS.

### Epitaph on Sophocles.

AROUND this place where Sophocles reclines,
  Let ivy silent creep, and fruitful vines ;
Let palm-trees overhang his honored tomb,
And flowering roses shed a sweet perfume.
Gifted with pleasant words and precepts wise,
Muses and Graces were his choice allies !

## THEOCRITUS.

### Epitaph on Hipponax.

A POET, Hipponax, here lies !
  His tomb the bad access denies ;
Honest and well born, here repose,
Or, if you wish, in quiet, doze !

## ANACREON.

TIMOCRITUS was brave, his tomb behold!
War spares the coward, sweeps away the bold.

———∘∘⋮●⋮∘∘———

## NOSSIS, THE LOCRIAN SAPPHO.

### ON A PORTRAIT.

MELINNA'S self is here portrayed,
In all her mother's charms arrayed.
The loving face and eyes, you see,
Turn as I turn, and follow me.
'Tis well to see the parent's grace
Reflected in the daughter's face!

———∘∘⋮●⋮∘∘———

## PLATO.

THEY speak but idly who Nine Muses own,
Showing that Sappho was to them unknown.

———————

### ANOTHER.

THEY idly speak, who speak of Muses Nine;
Behold a tenth in Sappho's glowing line!

## AUTHORS UNCERTAIN.

WHO, married once, seeks marriage-rites again,
Is like wrecked sailor daring twice the main !

———

THE rose's beauty in brief space is gone :
Seeking for roses, you find left a thorn !

———

ALCMEON was a bard, but not renowned ;
Nor was his head with laurel garlands crowned.
Alcman I have in mind, whose sounding lyre
First gave the Dorian chant impassioned fire !

———

ALTHOUGH remote from home you meet with death,
Be not disturbed, where'er you part with breath ;
From Athens — Meroe — the path is straight
To Charon's boat, to Pluto's gloomy gate !
To Hope and Fortune both, a long farewell !
A way I've found, nor with you care to dwell.

Rejoicing when poor mortals you deride,
You both may perish in your fickle pride.
For those things which are not, as in a dream,
You fain to us would make substantial seem.
Perish, thou wench, who woe for ever brings !
Perish, both trulls, well versed in cheating things !
Exert your talents on those left behind,
And those not wise you easily will find !

---

Lo ! Epicharmus crowned at home with fame,
As much his greater learning I proclaim
As the bright sun excels the starry train :
Others are streamlets, he the bounding main !

---

## PAULUS SILENTARIUS.

NOR fortune's favors hold in much respect,
     Nor let dark care thy freedom, ease, affect.
Hither and thither agitating strife
Of restless winds oppose the course of life.
Virtue is steadfast, has enduring throne,
Life's surging billows calmed by her alone.

### SILENTARIUS TO HIS FRIEND AGATHIAS.

LOVE does not fairly any law respect,
No other frenzy man can thus affect.
If by life's other cares thy soul is pressed,
Then love, all potent, dwells not in thy breast.
Though somewhat distant from thy virgin bride,
What is that love which lets the sea divide ?
Swimming, all reckless of the night's dark wave,
Leander proved that lovers' hearts were brave.
But no such trial, friend, your fates require :
Ships at your call, if transport you desire.
Pallas you worship, Venus would disarm :
Pallas has laws, but Venus passion's charm.
Where is the man, obeying Venus well,
Can shape his course, and with Minerva dwell ?

### ANTIPHILUS OF BYZANTIUM.

YE hanging branches of the oaks so tall,
   Whose lofty arms give grateful shade to all,
When, full of leaves, more dense than tilèd dome,
Your boughs at noontide make the cricket's home.
Escaping from the sun's full rays, with these
Let me enjoy your foliage, as I please.

### CRINAGORAS TO THE STATUE OF NERO.

THE works of Nero all the world control,
　　From East to West, from North to Southern
　　　　Pole !
O'er German nations vict'ries he has won,
And where Armenia hails the rising sun.
His strength in arms the wild Araxes knows,
And slaves who dwell where Rhine's fair water flows.

### ISIDORUS.

NOR storm, nor want of stars, nor Afric wave,
　　Sent our dear friend to such untimely grave.
All tranquil and serene, the ship confined,
They die of thirst, unaided by the wind.
How many evils mariners befall,
If breeze tempestuous, or if none at all !

### PHILODEMUS TO STATUE OF PAN.

IN this marble you may see
　　Not one God, but truly three.
There is here Herculean breast,
Head of Pan ; and, for the rest,

Hermes' legs and thighs are here.
Stranger, worship and revere !
For to three Gods joined in one
You can offer orison.

### DIONYSIUS.

WOULD I were Zephyr, you with heat oppressed
Obliged to court me to your panting breast !
Raised by your hand, borne to your breast of snow,
Would I were blushing rose thereon to glow !
Would I were lily fairest of the fair,
Placed in your bosom, but outrivalled there !

### MELEAGER.

BY Venus ! Cupid, I will burn your bow ;
Your quiver, arrows, in the fire will throw ;
All I will truly burn ; your wanton wiles
May end in laugh sardonic, though with smiles
From that flat nose so gayly you deride ;
If you cut off the wings of Love that guide,

Your feet with brazen fetters I will bind,
Although Cadmean vict'ry we may find ;
For if at home with courage I constrain,
My very herds will feel your hurtful reign.
Leave me, depart ! though hard to move I know,
Take sandals, on swift wings to others go.

SINGING cricket drunk with dews,
Chatty, lone, and rustic Muse !
To the tops of trees you draw
Your tawny body like a saw,
And you breathe a soft desire,
Sweet as music from the lyre.
As the wood-nymphs pass along,
Sing, my friend, new, sportive song,
And reply to father Pan,
Making all the noise you can,
When I seek the plane-tree shade,
When I fly, of Love afraid ;
Seeking there my peace to keep,
In a quiet noonday sleep.

## ANTIPATER OF SIDON.

### Inscription on the Tomb of Lais.

A MORTAL Venus here claims peaceful rest,
    Lais who dwelt on sea-bound Corinth's shore,
Charming in love, in gold and purple vest,
Pirene's fountain could not sparkle more.
There were proud suitors who her favors bought,
In number more than those who Helen sought;
Still from her mouth a racy flavor breathes,
And from her hair comes frankincense in wreaths;
Expanding flowers that bear a rich perfume,
Upspringing, cast a fragrance round her tomb.
Venus, outrivalled, tore her beauteous face,
And sighing Love bewailed such mournful case.
If her choice favors Lais had not sold,
For Greece ten years of toils, like those of old.

### Epitaph on Homer.

HERE Homer the divine hath found repose:
He sang of heroes and of Troja's woes.

6

## PHILLIPPUS OF THESSALONICA.

WHEN on the field Leonidas expired,
Xerxes with purple robe the chief attired ;
But the great hero speaking from the dead,
" Gifts due to traitors I refuse," he said ;
" Away with Persia's gifts !   To shades below,
Borne on my glorious shield, a Spartan I will go !"

## LUCIAN.

THE wealth that came to Theron by descent,
Menippus' son in youth had basely spent.
His father's friend Euctemon then became
Theron's protector, spite of his ill fame ;
Giving his daughter in her youthful charms,
With a large dowry, to the spendthrift's arms.
But Theron, though beyond all hope restored
From pinching poverty to plenteous board,
Was soon regardless of Euctemon's trust,
Indulged base appetite, relapsed to lust.
His wanton orgies brought a refluent wave,
And he was sunk, beyond all power to save.

Euctemon mourned, not now Menippus' son,
But for the nuptials, and the dowry gone.
At length discovered, what he should have known, —
*Another's he will waste who wastes his own.*

As if not long to live, thy goods enjoy;
Long life expecting, of expense be coy:
He is the wise man having both in view, —
Can spare, can spend, and temp'rate course pursue!

AND short is life when all things prosp'rous flow;
One night is long to those condemned to woe!

WHEN granting favor, grant the favor soon:
What's given coldly is not thought a boon.

### CLYTEMNESTRA TO ORESTES.

Do you intend with sword to pierce her through,
Whose frame produced, whose bosom nourished you?

FORTUNE is potent, though not always wise!
The proud abases, bids the lowly rise.

Although the gold to you in streams should flow,
Your pride and scorn may still receive a blow.
The wind attacks not herbs that grace the field,
But to its force tall oaks and plane-trees yield.

---

### LUCIAN OR ARCHIAS.

NOW Pan's mistress doth rejoice!
    Hear you not young Echo's voice?
Finding sport in every sound,
That the shepherds make around;
Hearing every thing you say,
If you linger in her way.

---

### MARIANUS.

WHERE parted earth the ocean doth divide,
    And sea-washed strait to shore is wand'ring
      wide,
A noble palace late the King Serene
Gave to Sophia, his much-honored Queen.
Shining in Europe, Asia sees the dome,
Worthy of thee, O King! and worthy Rome.

### To a Statue of Cupid crowned.

Where is that bow of yours, the wings, the dart,
And those sharp arrows meant to pierce the heart?
Why on your head a wreath, why garlands hold?
" Stranger, think not I am of common mould;
Not of the earth, nor son of earthly joy,
No common Venus owns me for her boy.
To the pure mind of man I send a flame,
And lead his soul to heaven, from whence it came;
Four garlands from the Virtues I entwine,
And, above all, the prize of Wisdom mine!"

### To the Grove called the Love Grove of Amasia.*

This Grove of Love hath charms; the western breeze
Sends soothing murmurs through the well-pruned
    trees;
On dewy meadow sparkling violets glow,
And from a triple source the waters flow;

---

* Amasia, capital of the kings of Pontus, the modern Amasiah.
The River Iris courses through the city.

In some of our country towns they have a Love Lane. It appears
that anciently they had Love Groves.

And here at noonday Iris rolls its wave,
That fair-haired wood-nymphs may at pleasure lave ;
Here fruitful vine and fertile olive bless,
Exposed on all sides to the Sun's caress ;
Here all around the nightingales are heard, —
Crickets responding to the tuneful bird.
Regard, my friend, a well-meant, kind request ;
Pass not my gate, — I welcome such a guest.

### ANOTHER BY THE SAME AUTHOR TO THE SAME GROVE.

COME, restless wanderer, to this Grove repair,
Refresh your frame and breathe this fragrant air !
'Mid plane-trees waters flow in wanton pride,
From many sources soothing streamlets glide ;
Dark purple violets the Spring supplies ;
In Summer, roses greet admiring eyes ;
The dewy meadows, with light slope inclined,
Present the ivy, branch with branch entwined ;
Through grassy banks the river circles round,
Girding a valley with rich foliage crowned.
What other name than Love befits a place
Where all is Beauty and where all is Grace !

## HARMODIUS AND ARISTOGITON.

To the Editor of the Boston Courier:

Having noticed your new translation of the "Harmodian melody," I send one for your critical consideration. Instead of "wreathed" I use "concealed," which, differing from other translations, requires explanation.

Harmodius and Aristogiton conspired with others to free Athens from the tyranny of the family of Pisistratus, intending at the great festival in honor of Minerva, called the Panathenæ, celebrated once in five years, to destroy Hippias, the actual tyrant, and his brother Hipparchus. At this festival the old men were accustomed to carry branches of olive in procession; the younger, branches of myrtle, — waving them as they passed to the Temple of Athene, who had the credit of being the founder of Athens, and whose temple there was one of magnificence.

Under the tyranny of Hippias, the citizens were not allowed to bear arms, except in religious processions as part of the pageant, and then only shields and spears. The conspirators planned to conceal a small sword, or more properly what we should call a dagger, in the branches of the myrtle-boughs it was the custom to carry. Seeing one of their number in familiar discourse with Hippias, the conspirators concluded they were betrayed; and, having personal cause of hate to Hipparchus, they hastened to kill him. Harmodius was also slain on the spot.

Hippias, when he heard of the death of Hipparchus, ordered all bearing arms to deposit them, and put to the question those discovered with daggers. The tyranny of Hippias continued about three years after : he was then exiled, and great honors were then paid to Harmodius and Aristogiton. Statues were erected, and the strain attributed to Callistratus written to celebrate their memory. This

melody was the Marseilles Hymn of the day; and the custom prevailed at Athens of singing the "Harmodian" at all convivialities,
those singing, waving branches of myrtle and passing them from one
to another, — a custom that continued as late as the time of Plutarch.

The impression the word "wreathed" gave me, when first reading
the strain many years ago, was that the myrtle was twined round the
sword as an ornament.

It is remarkable that Lord Denman should have mistaken the pur-
pose of the myrtle-branches, as Sir William Jones, in his Latin Lyric
to Liberty, expressly recognizes it : —

> "Quis myrtea ensem fronde reconditum
> Cantabit ? Illum civibus Harmodi
> Dilecte servatis."

In the Lysistrata of Aristophanes is a similar expression : —

> "Since I will be upon my guard, and bear
> The sword, henceforth hid in a myrtle branch,
> And in the forum, near Aristogiton,
> Appear," —

there being a column in honor of Aristogiton in the forum when
Aristophanes wrote, one hundred years after the death of Hipparchus.

In the Latin translation of the foregoing passage, by Jos. Scali-
ger, is —

> "Ensemque clausum fronde myrtea geram,"

and the Greek is the same used by Callistratus.

In the Acharnians of Aristophanes, in one place, the Lyric is
termed the "Harmodian melody;" and one threatens that another
shall not sing it with him, — that is, shall not be his companion at
feasts. In another place, when speaking of preparation for an in-
tended feast, the Lyric is called "the sweet Harmodian strain" : —

> "And all the rest is now in readiness,
> .  .  .  .  .  .  .  .  .  .
> Fair dancers, and the sweet Harmodian strain."

The history of the scolion is given in the introductory prelection of Dr. Lowth, in 1762, where it is said in a note, "Conjuratos, cum Hipparchum adorirentur, pugiones suos abdidisse in illis myrti ramis," which the commentator thinks were carried by those interested in the Panathenæ.

"Concealed" expresses the meaning, but "enwreathed" is more poetical and expresses the meaning better than "wreathed."

## CALLISTRATUS.

IN myrtle concealed this sword I will bear,
 Like Harmodius and Aristogiton the brave,
When the tyrant Hipparchus they slew,
 When just laws to Athens they gave.
Though long from this earth your spirit has fled,
 Beloved Harmodius ! you never were dead,
But with swift-footed Achilles, with Diomed, rest, —
 Translated, like them, to the Isles of the Blest !
My sword in myrtle concealed I will wave,
 Like those heroes so dear, those heroes so brave,
By whom, at Athene's magnificent fane,
 That man, the tyrant Hipparchus, was slain !
These heroes in glory immortal shall reign,
 For Justice prevailed, when the tyrant was slain.

## ALCÆUS.

Of the poet Alcæus, the inventor of the Alcaic measure, but few fragments remain. It seems to be understood that Horace was much indebted to him. In the Grecian Epigrams, Alcæus is ranked with Pindar, and was celebrated in early song as a high-toned patriot, was illustrious for his opposition to tyranny, and for the force and nobleness of his verse, for which he is greatly commended by Horace, and especially by Quintilian, for his verses written against tyrants.

Speaking of Alcæus, Athenæus says : "For this poet will be found to have been in the habit of drinking at every season and in every imaginable condition of affairs."

Sir William Jones found in Ælius Aristides the sentiment of Alcæus quoted, but not his verse. The Rhetorician simply says : By Themistocles alone, or with very few others, does this saying appear to be approved, which, though Alcæus formerly had produced, many afterwards claimed : 'Not stones, nor wood, nor the art of artisans, make a State ; but where men are who know how to take care of themselves, there are cities and walls.' The above is in the second volume of Jebb's edition of Aristides. Sir William Jones arranged the prose of Aristides as if written in verse by Alcæus, and from it made his paraphrase, " What constitutes a State ? "

In the first volume of Aristides is a similar sentiment in prose, which may be translated : "Neither walls, theatres, porches, nor senseless equipage, make States ; but men who are able to rely upon themselves." I have endeavored to give a literal translation in verse, embracing both these passages. You will judge whether, literally translated, it is not as forcible as the famous paraphrase.

The fragments of Alcæus are not only few, but abrupt. I send you a translation of most of them ; and having in view the character given of him as a patriot, and as being fond of wine, I have ventured to imagine what he wrote. What he wrote is translated as literally as possible, the part added is noted with quotation-marks. It must not be imagined that Alcæus, though a lover of wine, was a Bacchanal. The Greeks had a wine not intoxicating, but which had a pleasant, exhilarating effect, similar to the elevation experienced from a cup of Hyson tea, by persons not in the constant use of that cheering but not inebriating beverage.

The following fragments are found in Athenæus (and in Bergk, London and Leipsic, 1853). Most, if not all, have been translated, but not by an American hand.

It is rather remarkable that neither Bland, Merivale, nor any other of the moderns has alluded to the copious Greek Anthology edited by Eilhardo Lubin, as early as 1604. There is a royal octavo volume of over 1000 pages by Lubin, printed in 1604, dedicated to the most illustrious, most powerful Maurice, Landgrave of Hesse. The volume contains more than eighty authors, is divided into seven books. The poems are not fragments, though generally short pieces.

It should be understood that in framing the fragments the editors exercise a somewhat arbitrary power. Bergk *dicit*, "Carmen hoc ex variis fragmentis composui." And in translating such fragments the sense may be fairly given without especial regard to the editors' collocation.

### FRAGMENT FIRST.

#### ALCÆUS' ADVICE TO AN AGRICULTURIST.

BY no means plant a tree before the vine, —
  "For life's chief business is to have good wine."

### SECOND.

Fast descending is the rain,
Fierce the tempest on the plain,
All the rivers are concrete.
Let the fire the storm defeat,
Pile on wood to keep me warm,
On soft pillow rest my form.
Place sweet wine in plenty by,
We will then the storm defy.
" Let the earth drink up the rain,
Let it dash against the pane,
All its dashing shall be vain ;
Let all elemental life
Join in elemental strife ;
Calmly we will view the scene,
No dark care shall intervene.
With our minds attuned to ease,
What to us the wildest breeze,
Or the rage of warring seas ?
Nought the constant mind is swayed,
Though the world is disarrayed ;
Never fearing outward foes,
We securely will repose.

Doris, bring a cheering bowl, —
Let the storm at venture roll ;
Pile on wood to keep us warm,
We will then defy the storm."

### THIRD.

FEARLESS the cricket from the leaves sings shrill.
When thistles bloom, women are bent on ill ;
Men are unmanned when Sirius rules the hour,
And heads and knees own his relaxing power.
And when he burns, support thyself with wine :
Oppressive heat demands a draught divine.

### FOURTH.

LET us drink, while drink we can,
For a day is but a span :
Let us wait not for a light ;
Come, we will forestall the night.
Bring rare cups of varied hues,
Such as Bacchus' self might choose ;
Fill the goblets to the brim,
When we drink a health to him.
Pour the wine by Jove's son given,
Care forgot, and earth is heaven.

Soon as one glass then is gone,
Doris, bring another on.
" And the wine we call dark Greek,
Wine that makes the dumb to speak,
Freely pass to all around,
Till all hearts with mirth abound ;
Drinking this, the circling blood
Cannot flow in sluggish flood ;
But all vapors disappear,
And the mind's left bright and clear."


### FIFTH.

Hail, Pan ! renowned Arcadia controlling ;
    Hail, Pan ! with dancing Bacchus well allied ;
In joyful strains exulting sing to me,
    The gracious gods gave victory to our side.
We conquered, as we wished, sustained by all the
    gods that we revere,
From Pandrosos, the all-refreshing, to Athene, ever
    dear.

### SIXTH.

With brass my spacious mansion shineth bright,
With crests of horse-hair flowing fair and white ;

And glittering helmets on my walls in line,
Designed for heroes, ornamental shine;
See splendid greaves that hidden nails enclose,
Which sure defence to strongest arms oppose;
Breast-plates and purest linen; hollow shields,
By cowards thrown away on battle-fields;
And many girdles; and Chalcidian swords;
And warlike garments, — these my pen records,
As first among the spoils by me acquired,
When martial ardor first my bosom fired.

### SEVENTH.

Nor porches, theatres, nor stately halls,
Nor senseless equipage, nor lofty walls,
Nor towers of wood or stone, nor workmen's arts,
Compose a State; but men with daring hearts,
Who on themselves rely to meet all calls,
Compose a State, — it needs not other walls!

### EIGHTH.

FIERCELY now the wave advancing,
   Sea of trouble it will bring;
And the ship is madly dancing,        .
   "And her timbers moaning sing:

Now the ship forlorn is riding,
   Who her courses now can keep?
Who the pilot that is guiding
   This vext bark upon the deep?
Rudderless, she now is dashing
   Onward, to a rock-bound shore,
Where the waves, in fury lashing,
   Echo ocean's sullen roar!
Behold, she plunges reckless on:
   Will she ever harbor bring?
With sails and masts and rudder gone,
   Round us seabirds dirges sing.
From what source can come salvation?
   Lo, the night still darker grows,
Who can save this sinking nation
   From accumulating woes?
See a country over-laden
   With injustice it should spurn!
Hail, Astrea, star-bright maiden!
   Come! to earth again return.
But the virgin could not tarry
   With these wreckers at the helm;
For the burthens that they carry
   Any bark would overwhelm!"

### NINTH.

WHENCE these winds impetuous blow
Is not in my gift to know ;
One wave in another lost,
Our dark ship 'mid ocean tost,
O'er our noble deck the sea
Seems to sweep triumphantly.
We drag anchor, and the sail,
Already rent, begins to fail.
" All the labors of the builders,
   All the beauty they bestowed,
Is in peril from this tempest ;
   And the worst we may forebode.
Those who owned the bark have trusted
   To a banded pirate crew :
Now, the keel already broken,
   What remains for us to do ?
Are we men, and ask the question ?
   Did we ever freedom prize ?
Where the compact that would bind us
   To be victimized by spies ?
If there's spirit left, or manhood,
   In our country, men will rise,

And throw off degrading fetters
  Forged by knaves they should despise.
Wake, then, from a fatal slumber !
  Swear, by all your sacred fanes,
That the future shall not see you
  Basely hugging servile chains !
Awake ! arise, lose not a moment,
  Let not despots hold the reins ;
Once the country had protectors,
  Who released you from your chains.
Save, O save, the bark from ruin,
  Though the winds and waters rave !
If you cannot live in freedom,
  Earn at least a storied grave ! "

Cambridge: Press of John Wilson and Son.